D0384914

A Note to Parents and Teachers

Kids can imagine, kids can laugh and kids can learn to read with this exciting new series of first readers. Each book in the Kids Can Read series has been especially written, illustrated and designed for beginning readers. Humorous, easy-to-read stories, appealing characters and engaging illustrations make for books that kids will want to read over and over again.

To make selecting a book easy for kids, parents and teachers, the Kids Can Read series offers three levels based on different reading abilities:

Level 1: Kids Can Start to Read

Short stories, simple sentences, easy vocabulary, lots of repetition and visual clues for kids just beginning to read.

Level 2: Kids Can Read with Help

Longer stories, varied sentences, increased vocabulary, some repetition and visual clues for kids who have some reading skills, but may need a little help.

Level 3: Kids Can Read Alone

Longer, more complex stories and sentences, more challenging vocabulary, language play, minimal repetition and visual clues for kids who are reading by themselves.

With the Kids Can Read series, kids can enter a new and exciting world of reading!

Sam's Snowy Day

Written by Mary Labatt

Illustrated by Marisol Sarrazin

Kids Can Press

™ Kids Can Read is a trademark of Kids Can Press Ltd.

Text © 2005 Mary Labatt
Illustrations © 2005 Marisol Sarrazin

All rights reserved. No part of this publication may be reproduced, stored in a retrieval system or transmitted, in any form or by any means, without the prior written permission of Kids Can Press Ltd. or, in case of photocopying or other reprographic copying, a license from The Canadian Copyright Licensing Agency (Access Copyright). For an Access Copyright license, visit www.accesscopyright.ca or call toll free to 1-800-893-5777.

Kids Can Press acknowledges the financial support of the Government of Ontario, through the Ontario Media Development Corporation's Ontario Book Initiative; the Ontario Arts Council; the Canada Council for the Arts; and the Government of Canada, through the BPIDP, for our publishing activity.

Published in Canada by
Kids Can Press Ltd.
29 Birch Avenue
Toronto, ON M4V 1E2

Published in the U.S. by
Kids Can Press Ltd.
2250 Military Road
Tonawanda, NY 14150

www.kidscanpress.com

Edited by David MacDonald
Designed by Marie Bartholomew
Printed and bound in China

The hardcover edition of this book is smyth sewn casebound.
The paperback edition of this book is limp sewn with a drawn-on cover.

CM 05 0 9 8 7 6 5 4 3 2 1
CM PA 05 0 9 8 7 6 5 4 3 2 1

Library and Archives Canada Cataloguing in Publication

Labatt, Mary, [date]

Sam's snowy day / written by Mary Labatt ; illustrated by Marisol Sarrazin.

(Kids Can read)
ISBN 1-55337-789-3 (bound). ISBN 1-55337-790-7 (pbk.)

I. Sarrazin, Marisol, 1965– II. Title. III. Series: Kids Can read (Toronto, Ont.)

PS8573.A135S26 2005 jC813'.54 C2004-906568-8

Kids Can Press is a Corus™ Entertainment company

3 3097 06513 4840

Sam woke up and looked outside.

Everything was white!

The roofs were white.

The grass was white.

The car was white.

"What is this?" thought Sam.

Sam ran to get Joan and Bob.

She went back to the window.

"Woof!" said Sam. "Woof, woof!"

Joan and Bob laughed.

“It’s snow, Sam!” said Bob.

“You will like snow.”

“What is snow?” thought Sam.

Joan and Bob put on coats and hats.

Then they put on mittens and boots.

“Let’s go out and play,” said Joan.

She opened the door.

Sam stuck her foot in the snow
and picked it up fast.
"Brrr," thought Sam.
"Snow makes my feet cold."

Sam stuck her nose in the snow

and sniffed.

"A-a-a-choo!" said Sam.

"Snow gets in my nose," she thought.

Sam stuck her tongue in the snow

and licked.

“Hmmm,” thought Sam.

“Snow tastes like water.”

“Let’s go to the park,” said Joan.

“We can have fun at the park.”

Bob got the toboggan.

"Hop on, Sam," said Bob.

Joan and Bob pulled Sam to the park.

Sam saw lots of people in the park.

People were making snowmen.

Kids were playing in the snow.

“Wow!” thought Sam.

“This is good!”

"Look," said Bob.

"They are making snow angels."

“I can do that,” thought Sam.

She lay down and waved her legs.

Sam got up to look.

It did not look like an angel.

Kids were throwing snowballs.

"I like balls," thought Sam.

She jumped to catch a snowball.

Splat!

The snowball hit Sam.

“Poor puppy,” said the kids.

Kids were sliding on the ice.

“I like to slide,” thought Sam.

She ran to slide with the kids.

Oof!

Sam slipped on the ice.

"Poor puppy," said the kids.

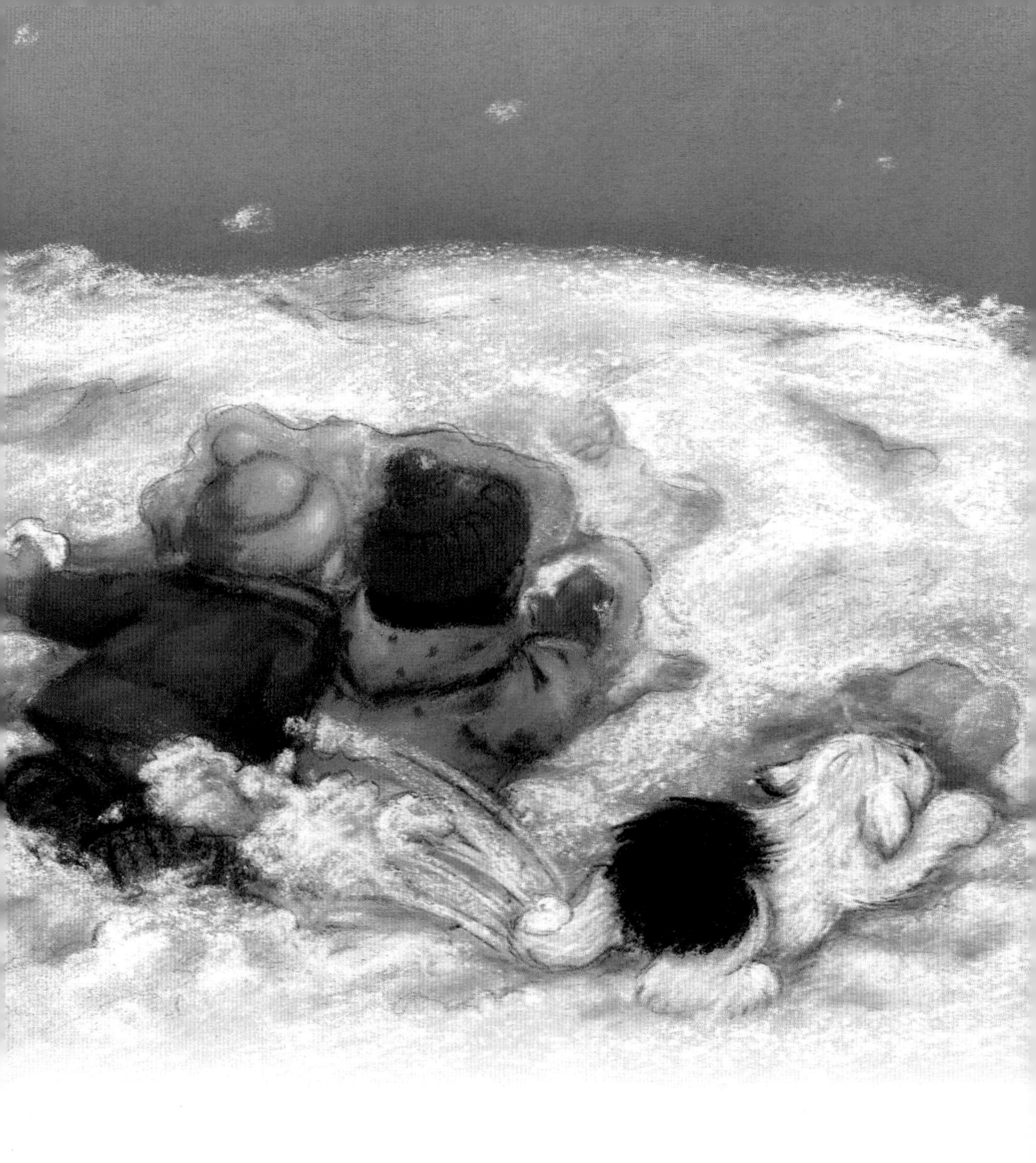

Kids were digging in the snow.

“I like to dig,” thought Sam.

She ran to dig with the kids.

Wump!

The snow fell on Sam.

"Poor puppy," said the kids.

Then Sam saw a hill.

Kids were riding on toboggans.

"Come on, puppy," said the kids.

"Hop on!"

Sam hopped on with the kids.

Down they went.

"Eeeeek!" cried the kids.

"Woof! Woof!" said Sam.

"Come on, puppy," said the kids.

"Let's go back up!"

Sam went back up the hill with the kids.

Down they came,

faster and faster,

faster and faster!

"Eeeeek!" cried all the kids.

"Woof! Woof! Woof!" said Sam.

No one saw the snowman in the way.

"Jump off!" yelled Joan and Bob.

All the kids jumped off.

"Not me!" thought Sam.

"I like this ride!"

WUMP!

The toboggan hit the snowman.

"Oh, no!" cried Joan and Bob.

"Where is the puppy?" cried the kids.

Sam wiggled out of the snow.

"I am not a puppy," she thought.

"I am a snowman!"